W9-BYH-408

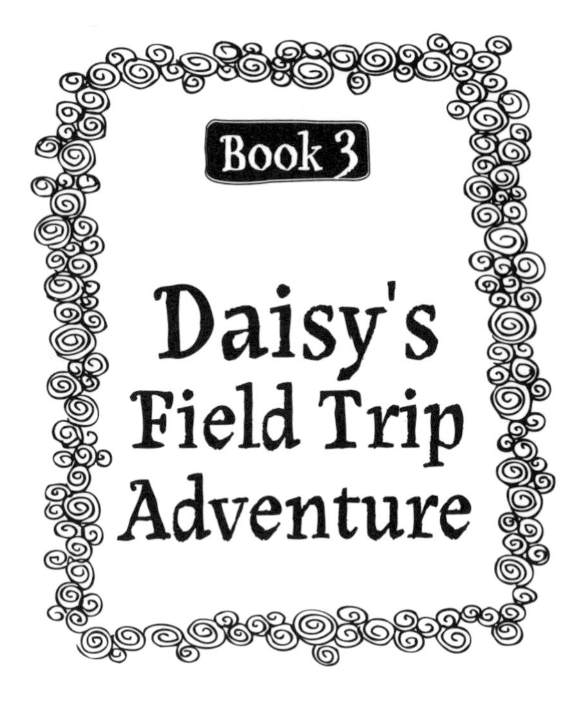

Book 3

Daisy's Field Trip Adventure

By: Marci Peschke

Illustrated by: M.H. Pilz

visit us at www.abdopublishing.com

To Para Mis Amigas: Amy, Kathleen & Cathy - MP
For Cole - MHP

Published by Magic Wagon, a division of the ABDO Group, 8000 West 78th Street, Edina, Minnesota 55439.

Printed in the United States of America, Melrose Park, Illinois.
082010
012011
This book contains at least 10% recycled materials.

Original text by Marci Peschke
Illustrated by M.H. Pilz
Edited by Stephanie Hedlund and Rochelle Baltzer
Cover and interior design by Abbey Fitzgerald

Library of Congress Cataloging-in-Publication Data

Peschke, M. (Marci)
Daisy's field trip adventure / by Marci Peschke ; illustrated by M.H. Pilz.
p. cm. -- (Growing up Daisy ; bk. 3)
ISBN 978-1-61641-116-9
[1. School field trips--Fiction. 2. Schools--Fiction. 3. Mexican Americans--Fiction.] I. Pilz, MH, ill. II. Title.
PZ7.P441245Dcg 2011
[Fic]--dc22

2010028459

Table of Contents

1 Go Fish!

The board in room 210 had a giant eye on it. That eye was staring right at Daisy Martinez!

"What is it? What's it for?" Daisy's best friend Blanca asked.

Daisy thought about their mysterious teacher, Ms. Lilly. Last week, Ms. Lilly wrote *Field Trip Next Week* on the board.

Then, Daisy carefully looked at the giant eye. She said, "It's a clue! I just know it is!"

Jason was just thinking the same thing. "Do you think we are going to study Greek myths?" he asked. "It reminds me of a cyclops."

Daisy and her classmates were fourth graders at Townsend Elementary School. They were lucky enough to have Ms. Lilly, the "new" teacher. Ms. Lilly was a super fun teacher!

Daisy looked at Jason and said, "Oh, I thought it was a field trip clue!"

Everyone in the room was talking when Ms. Lilly arrived. She was carrying a gigantic straw bag and she quickly stuffed it under her desk.

"Good morning, my super smart, superstar students. Are you ready to learn something new?" she said.

Raymond said, "Yup, like why is that eye up there?"

Ms. Lilly just laughed. Then she said, "Raymond, you are sooo clever to notice my artwork."

Blanca whispered, "Yeah right, who could miss it?"

Daisy raised her hand. When Ms. Lilly called on her she said, "Ms. Lilly, Jason and I are wondering if it's a clue of some kind?"

Ms. Lilly smiled. "Kudos, kudos, kudos, kiddos!" she exclaimed. "It is a clue and that's all I can tell you for now." Then she wrote in large letters on the other side of the board: *Poetry loves words*.

Ms. Lilly told the class they would be studying poetry all week long. She announced they would each have a poetry pal.

Blanca leaned across the aisle and whispered, "Hey, Daisy, let's be pals."

Just as Daisy nodded yes, Ms. Lilly pulled a round, glass fishbowl out of her straw bag. She pushed the bowl to the front of her desk and asked, "Is everyone ready to go fishing? I mean fishing for a poetry pal."

Daisy heard Jason groan. Jason was a brainiac. He earned all A's and never wanted to work with a partner.

Ms. Lilly called, "Row one, come on down!" Lizzie was the first one to pull a name. She pulled out Amber's name. Everyone liked Amber. She was nice.

Two more kids went fishing and then it was Daisy's turn. She had been chanting quietly, "Let it be Blanca, let it be Blanca." Daisy shoved her hand in the bowl and swirled it around three times. Usually three was one of her lucky numbers.

Daisy pulled out the small, folded paper. She held her breath as she slowly opened it. She saw neat black letters that spelled trouble!

Actually the letters on the paper were M-a-d-i-s-o-n. Daisy was nervous. She would be okay with it, but Madison could be snotty sometimes.

Ms. Lilly was waiting. She said, "Daisy, what kind of fish did you get? Who is on your paper?"

Daisy wanted to say she got a stinky fish, but that wouldn't be nice. Besides, sometimes she liked Madison. Instead she said, "I've got Madison."

From the other side of the room Madison said, "Nooo! Ms. Lilly, do I have to have Daisy as my poetry pal? Can't she choose again? I really think Lizzie should be my pal."

Ms. Lilly said, "Madison, Lizzie already has a pal, but I'll let Daisy throw her fish back in the bowl if you insist."

Daisy sighed with relief. She swished her hand in the fish bowl three times and pulled a

new name. It was Blanca! She thought, *Three really is my lucky number this time!*

The rest of the row continued to fish for names, but Daisy and Blanca hardly noticed. They were busy celebrating the fact that they were going to work together.

When it was Raymond's turn, he pulled out a paper and gave it to Ms. Lilly. She read it and then announced the name, "Madison."

From across the room, Daisy could see Madison's face was bright red like a chili pepper, but she didn't say anything. Ms. Lilly had already allowed Madison one chance to get another partner.

Daisy felt sorry for Madison and for Raymond. She didn't think they would like working together. For one thing, Raymond didn't usually do his work.

Raymond shuffled back to his seat and sat down. Ms. Lilly said, "We are making a

poetry portfolio. We are doing several poetry assignments that you can include. Let's begin."

Then she wrote on the board: *Ms. Lilly loves to linger licking a luscious lemonade lollipop.*

Ms. Lilly explained that alliteration was using a bunch of words that started with the same sound in a row.

"For this assignment, poetry pals will write an alliteration sentence about each other," she said. "You have five minutes and then we'll share your sentences. Start!"

Amber was chewing on her pencil. Jason was thinking. Daisy wrote: *Beautiful Blanca blinks at the big butterfly blanket covering her backyard.*

Blanca wrote: *Darling Daisy draws delightful doodles during December.*

After they finished their sentences, Daisy and Blanca traded to read what the other had written.

"Ooooh! I love it!" Blanca said.

"Blanca, you're the best. Hey, that's alliteration!" Daisy said.

When it was time to read the sentences to the whole class, Raymond raised his hand to read his right away.

Ms. Lilly said, "Okay, Raymond, get us started." Everyone was surprised since Raymond hardly ever did his class work. He cleared his throat.

Ms. Lilly said, "Raymond, please stand. Everyone, pencils down, pay attention, and honor the reader."

Raymond stood up. He said, "Monster Madison makes mischief mashing mangos on Mars."

No one said anything, but Madison looked mad. Ms. Lilly said, "Raymond, you did understand the assignment but made a mistake. We never use names like ***monster***

when talking about our classmates. Could you please change your sentence?"

Raymond looked confused. He said, "I already wrote it right."

Ms. Lilly said, "Raymond, please consider changing ***monster*** to ***martian***."

Raymond erased something on his paper. Then he said, "Madison, I guess you are a martian instead of a monster."

Madison's face was red again. She read her sentence, "Raymond the rude rarely reads."

Ms. Lilly's face turned as red as her nail polish. She said, "Madison, my office pronto!" She was already walking toward the door. That meant they were going to the hall.

Madison was in terrible trouble!

The kids tried their hardest to hear their teacher talking in the hall. But, no sounds passed through the heavy wood door.

Moments later, Madison pushed the door open. She walked right up to Raymond and said, "I am truly sorry, Raymond."

Raymond just shrugged. Ms. Lilly asked, "Class, do we need a lesson on kindness?" Everyone said, "No!"

The rest of the sentences were sweet, or funny, or wacky, but there were no more mean ones. Once all the sentences were read, it was time to go to gym class.

Ms. Lilly's class lined up to go to the gym. On the way through the halls, Daisy saw her

younger brothers, Manuel and Diego. They were too busy making faces at each other to notice her.

Daisy thought that sisters were much nicer. She loved her younger sister Paola and her baby sister Carmen.

As they got close to the gym they heard loud music. Ms. Lilly's class had gym with Mr. Harrison's fourth grade class. Usually, Coach Cervantes had the classes do a quick warm-up in long rows. Then she gave out instructions. The person at the front of each row was a leader for the week.

But today they were going to start playing volleyball. They couldn't stand in rows because Coach had already set up the volleyball nets.

When everyone was in the gym, Coach turned off the music, whistled, and said, "Okay, line up along the walls and we'll choose teams for volleyball. First, I need to choose some captains."

Coach Cervantes looked around the gym. Then, she shouted, "DeShaye, Amber, Wes, and Eric are our captains!"

DeShaye was one of Daisy's closest friends, and she and Wes were in Mr. Harrison's class. Eric was in Daisy's class, but he never said much. He was sporty like DeShaye. Amber and Wes were not that good at sports.

"Okay," Coach said. "Let's choose teams. In volleyball, each team gets six players including the captain."

Daisy hated waiting to get picked for a team. No one wanted to be the last person picked. DeShaye picked Daisy, Blanca, Pablo, Cameron, and David.

Daisy looked around. The last kid to get picked was Raymond. Eric didn't want him, but he was the only kid left.

As Coach began to show them how to serve DeShaye said, "Hey, I serve all the time when I play tennis."

Coach Cervantes explained that it was different in volleyball, because you didn't have a racket. It still seemed to DeShaye that they were a lot alike. Everyone took turns serving the ball.

Daisy found out she was pretty good at serving. She might even decide that volleyball was fun.

Then Coach said, "Tomorrow, you'll learn to pass the ball. Then, I'll teach you about blocking."

Madison groaned. She hated gym. She was on Amber's team, but Lizzie was on Wes's team. Daisy was glad Madison and Raymond were not on the same team. She was still thinking about how mean Madison had been to him.

The classes both lined up to wait for their teachers. Ms. Lilly was right on time, but Mr. Harrison was late.

On the way back to class, Daisy could hear Madison telling Lizzie that Coach Cervantes

was mean. Madison was in a bad mood because she didn't get to be on a team with Lizzie.

Daisy was super glad to be on a team with her friends. She felt sorry for Raymond, but he didn't seem to care that no one wanted him on their team.

She slipped back to the end of the line by Raymond. She asked, "Raymond, do you want me to help you practice your volleyball serve at recess today?"

"Yeah, sure," Raymond said with a big smile. Daisy was hoping DeShaye would help, too!

Back in room 210, sky blue paper with clouds on it was waiting on everyone's desks. Ms. Lilly said, "We have a little time before lunch, so everyone get out your book and read. I will explain the cloud paper assignment when we get back from lunch."

The class quieted down and every kid pulled out a book and began to read. Daisy absolutely adored books. It seemed like she

had just started to read when Ms. Lilly called, "Yum-o, kiddos, lunchtime."

The lunch room was noisy! Kids were complaining because it was meat loaf day.

"Gross," Daisy said. "I'm glad I bring my lunch every day. I have ***tamales*** today. My ***abuela*** made them."

Daisy's abuela lived with her family and helped with the kids and the cooking.

Blanca said, "You are soooo lucky!"

DeShaye pushed the mystery meat around on her tray.

"You can have some of my fried rice," Min said to DeShaye. She held out her chopsticks to her friend.

Blanca didn't even ask Daisy for a bite of the tamales. She just dug right in with her fork. The new principal was walking around the cafeteria. He stopped to ask how the lunch was.

"Principal Donaldson," DeShaye said, "if you can get this brown goo off of the lunch menu, we'll all do extra homework for a month."

The principal looked uncomfortable and asked, "That bad, huh?"

Blanca scooted closer to the end of the table. She said, "It's way worse than bad. It's totally disgusting. I bet even a cockroach wouldn't eat it."

Principal Donaldson promised to prepare a new, improved monthly menu with the help of Ms. Pearl, who was the head of the cafeteria.

Raymond, who has been quiet all along, said, "The food's not that bad."

"Yeah, right!" Blanca said. Then she threw her meat loaf in the trash.

When Ms. Lilly picked up the class from the cafeteria, she was holding a pile of old quilts stacked so high the kids couldn't even see her head. They knew it was their teacher because of the red nail polish.

“Class, please follow me,” they heard her muffled voice say. Daisy scooted up beside Ms. Lilly and asked, “Can I help carry some quilts?”

Madison was right behind her and said, “Me too.” Ms. Lilly seemed happy to let the students help.

“Our destination is the soccer field,” Ms. Lilly said. Eric suddenly acted interested. He asked, “Are we gonna play some soccer today?” Ms. Lilly told him to be patient.

When they finally walked out on the field, Ms. Lilly told them to shake out the quilts and put them on the ground. As the colorful quilts blew out into the wind and floated to the ground, they looked like butterfly wings.

Their teacher told the boys to lie down on the quilts on her right side and the girls to lie

down on the quilts on her left side. The she flopped back on a quilt, too.

"Observe the clouds, my superstar students," Ms. Lilly said. "Memorize the shifting shapes you see, because we are going to write cloud poems."

Jason shouted, "I see a rocket ship!"

Daisy said, "It looks more like the Eiffel Tower to me."

Raymond didn't say anything. Blanca was going on and on about a cloud that looked like a castle. Then the clouds beside it shifted and formed a dragon.

Eric said, "Whoa dude, that dragon is going to crush your cloud castle."

Ms. Lilly said, "I see a train. Do you see the engine and the small clouds are like train cars? Trains make me think of my travels. I just love trains!"

Amber noticed a cloud that looked like a frog. Way too soon Ms. Lilly said, "Well, I think we have some ideas for our poems. Everyone, please help shake out the quilts and fold them. It's time to go inside."

When they got back inside, Ms. Lilly explained that the students should use notebook paper to write a draft of a cloud poem. Then, Ms. Lilly would check the poems. She would let the students who were ready type their poem and print it on the fabulous fluffy cloud paper.

The class would have until Wednesday to finish their poems. Daisy was already making some notes about the clouds she saw. She couldn't wait to tell her family about the interesting day in room 210.

At dinner that night, the Martinez kids were talking about their day at *escuela*. The boys were excited about Coach Cervantes and her volleyball lesson.

"I still like soccer best though," Manuel said.

"We can play both! Right?" Diego said.

Paola was talking about a science experiment in Ms. Wall's class. She said, "It was really fun and all the kids in my class got to make some green goo."

"No fair!" Manuel shouted. "I want to make green goo, too!"

Daisy said, "There was a mysterious eye on the board in my classroom today. Ms. Lilly wouldn't tell us what it means. I think it's a clue!"

Abuela said, "Pass the *frijoles, por favor*. What are you studying now, *mi ja*?"

Daisy told her grandmother that today they were writing poems. But, she didn't think the eye was a poetry clue.

"There could be a poem about a magic eye," Abuela said.

Everyone at the table was quiet. After a few seconds Paola said, "Maybe?"

Diego shouted, "No way!"

"Who is doing dishes tonight?" Papi asked. Paola and Daisy began to quickly clear the bright, colorful plates. Abuela helped Mami put the leftover food away.

When the chores were done, Mami went to take a bath, and Papi played with Carmen. Abuela sat down at the table with Daisy and hummed a little song.

"I used to write poems in Mexico a long, long time ago when I was a girl," she said. "*Oh, como me gustan las palabras*. If you have homework for the poems, then I will help you!"

Daisy said, "I have to write a cloud poem for homework." Abuela told Daisy to start by closing her eyes and thinking about the clouds she saw earlier that day. Daisy thought that was a great idea.

Paola said, "I'm going to write a cloud poem, too!"

Daisy smiled. Paola would probably end up watching television. Daisy got busy writing. First, she closed her eyes and remembered the white, puffy clouds. Then, she grabbed her pencil and wrote:

Cloud Castles

I am tiny as I watch the blue, blue sky

The clouds float above me very high

Towers, trains, and rocket ships

Castles and dragons with fire for lips

I gaze amazed by creamy cool clouds

They are white puffs of magical changing shapes!

When she finished the poem, she took it to Abuela, who was sitting in her big green chair in the living room.

"Abuela, can you read my poem?" Daisy asked. Abuela smiled as she took the paper. After a moment she looked up and put her arm around Daisy.

"*¡Muy hermoso!*" Abuela said. "You have a gift for the words just like your abuela."

Then Mami came in the room and asked, "Is your homework finished, Daisy?" Before Daisy could answer her, Abuela told Mami to read the cloud poem.

"Daisy, you are a brilliant writer," Mami said. "I am so proud of you! Now, will you make sure Paola takes her bath and brushes her teeth?"

Daisy took her poem from Mami. She said, "*Sí,* Mami." Then she gave Abuela and Mami both a big hug.

The next day at school everyone in room 210 got a big surprise! Ms. Lilly began to collect the cloud poems, but suddenly everyone heard *meow . . . meow*.

"Hey!" Raymond said. "It sounds like there's a cat in here!"

Madison shouted, "I'm a dog lover!"

Daisy was busy listening to the meowing. She was trying to figure out where the noise was coming from. It sounded like it was right under Ms. Lilly's desk.

"It sounds like a real cat!" Amber said. Just then, a light brown cat with sky blue eyes, big ears, and a black tail peered around the corner of the desk.

"I knew it!" Daisy exclaimed. "Is it your cat, Ms. Lilly? Please tell us her name."

Ms. Lilly walked to her desk and scooped up the cat. She said, "Quite right. She is my cat and her name is Cleo. She will come to you if she wants to meet you. She doesn't use her sharp teeth to bite. But when she is not happy instead of *meow* she will say *yeow*!"

Ms. Lilly put Cleo down. Cleo sat quietly while Ms. Lilly picked up the rest of the papers.

Jason had a puzzled look on his face. Ms. Lilly noticed and asked, "Jason, do you have a question?"

Jason suddenly got a huge smile on his face. "No, ma'am," he said. "I just figured it out. The cat is a clue!"

Ms. Lilly shouted, "Bingo! And I think it is only fair to tell you that Cleo is not her full name. She is a Siamese cat and very proud of her name. It is, in fact, a rather royal name."

Just then Cleo decided to jump up on Daisy's desk. Daisy felt a swish of fur as Cleo made herself comfortable. Looking at Cleo up close, Daisy noticed a black and gold collar with weird-looking designs all around it. She thought she could see a bird and—wait! It looked like an eye, a familiar eye. One like Ms. Lilly drew on the board yesterday.

Now I have a private clue, she thought. She hoped no one else would notice the strange collar.

Ms. Lilly was ready to begin the poetry lesson, so she waved a long stick with a red feather on the end and Cleo jumped down from Daisy's desk. The cat walked slowly toward the feather

pretending not to notice. When she was close, she pounced on the feather, trying to grab it between her paws.

Ms. Lilly ignored Cleo completely. She was busy asking the class to write their favorite color on a piece of paper.

Daisy could tell that Jason was still thinking about the clue. He was staring into space. She was still thinking about the clue, too.

Next, Ms. Lilly asked the class to list all of the things that were their favorite color. Daisy saw Blanca had ***pink*** written on her paper.

Blanca leaned over and asked, "What color are you going to choose, Daisy?"

Daisy wrote ***blue*** on her paper and held it up so Blanca could see. Blanca gave her a thumbs-up.

Daisy listed on her paper: sky, lakes, flowers, feelings, blueberries, cotton candy, jeans, eyes, bird eggs, and beach glass. She had a bracelet

made out of frosty bits of broken glass she found on the beach over the summer.

She noticed that Blanca had bubble gum and fairy wands on her pink list. Ms. Lilly was walking around the room looking at everyone's list. She had a gigantic box of crayons. There were hundreds of colors in the box.

Ms. Lilly handed the box to each student and told them to choose a crayon that was their favorite color. Daisy picked periwinkle. Blanca picked razzle dazzle rose.

Then she heard Ms. Lilly ask, "Raymond, are you sure you want black?"

"Yup, black is my favorite color," Raymond said. The class spent the afternoon writing color poems. It was really fun!

Ms. Lilly let them write the poems in colored marker, then illustrate them or cut out pictures from old magazines and paste them around their poems.

Principal Donaldson came in with a notepad and looked around. The kids hardly noticed him. They were busy working on their poems. Even Raymond seemed to really like the assignment.

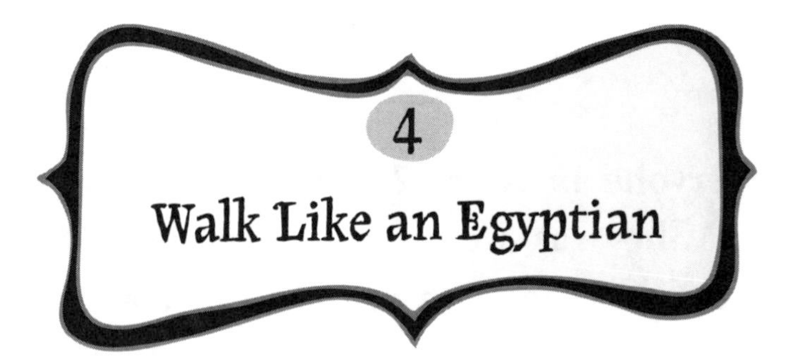

On Wednesday, Daisy met Blanca in the hall by their lockers. She shouted, "I know what the eye means!"

Then she realized that in her excitement she was shouting. She put her finger over her lips.

Blanca whispered, "I'll keep it a secret."

Daisy explained Cleo's special cat collar. Then, she told Blanca that she looked up the strange symbols on the computer at home.

"Blanca, they're Egyptian," Daisy said. "And I'm betting Cleo's name is really *Cleopatra* after the famous Queen of Egypt. You know what that means . . ."

"King Tut!" both girls shouted together.

Daisy said, "Sssh." Then the five minute bell rang.

Everyone in room 210 was staring at Ms. Lilly. She was wearing a long white dress, gold sandals, and ton of gold bracelets. Her eyes had a lot of dark makeup on them and her beautiful curly black hair was straight as a board.

"Hey, who are you supposed to be?" Raymond asked.

"I think I know!" Daisy announced as she sat down.

Ms. Lilly said, "Who do you think I am, Daisy?"

"I think you are Cleopatra, Queen of Egypt," Daisy answered. "And, I think we are going to see King Tut on our field trip. Am I right?"

Jason chimed in. He said, "I think you are only half right, Daisy."

Ms. Lilly said, "You are a super smart superstar, Jason! Now tell everyone who I am."

Jason explained that Daisy was on the right track. He said, "Yesterday I noticed that Ms. Lilly's cat had a special collar with symbols called hieroglyphics on it. So, I went home and did some research."

Daisy said, "Me too!"

Jason told the class that at first he thought it was going to be Cleopatra, too. Then he used logic to determine that they were going to see the King Tut exhibit for their field trip.

Daisy said, "Me too!"

Jason said, "I just kept digging and I found out Tut's mother was Nefertiti. She was one of the most beautiful women in the ancient world. I'm guessing Ms. Lilly is the beautiful Nefertiti. Am I right?"

When Jason realized what he'd said, his face went red all the way up to the roots of his hair. He looked like he had sunburn.

Ms. Lilly clapped her hands with delight. She bowed in Jason's direction and said, "You are correct, young scholar."

Daisy said, "Then we are going to see King Tut on the field trip and I was half right?"

Ms. Lilly said, "So true, Daisy!"

Next Ms. Lilly gave every student a copy of a book called *The Egypt Game*.

"Students, you will all love this mystery!" Ms. Lilly said. "It has Nefertiti in it. I'm going to put you in groups of three."

Ms. Lilly then went around the room with a wooden box. Each student pulled out an Egyptian symbol from the box. When everyone had a paper Ms. Lilly said, "Find the two other students whose papers have a matching symbol."

In moments, all of the kids were running around the room trying to find their group.

Madison kept shouting, "Who has a bird? Who has a bird?"

Eric was shouting, "Maddy wants a cracker! Maddy wants a cracker!"

Ms. Lilly tapped him on the shoulder and he stopped.

Amber said, "I have a bird." Jason looked at it and told her it was a vulture. He also looked at Madison's paper. It was a vulture, too!

Madison said, "Ms. Lilly, I can't be a vulture!"

"Yes, you can," Amber said. "Lizzie is a vulture, too."

Jason was an owl and that seemed just right. Blanca was a rabbit and so was Raymond.

Daisy was a cobra. The cobra was the symbol for a queen or a goddess, which was the reason Eric didn't want to be in Daisy's group!

Lola had a cobra, too. That meant Eric, Daisy, and Lola were in a group. Ms. Lilly said each group could choose a project. Then she wrote several options on the board.

The class could choose from: make a map of ancient Egypt, design an Egyptian art display, create a table of information on Egyptian artifacts, or use hieroglyphics to make names or words.

Jason said, "The owls are doing hieroglyphics. I know a lot about them already."

Ms. Lilly said, "Your group can decide *together* to do any of the projects. They will be due next Friday."

Daisy's group decided to create a map of ancient Egypt. Each group had thirty minutes of class time to plan their project.

When the thirty minutes were up, Ms. Lilly said, "Class, we need to speak about our field trip next Friday."

Eric and Amber passed out permission slips while Madison and Lizzie passed out a letter. Ms. Lilly explained that the letter was an invitation from Queen Nefertiti, aka Ms. Lilly, for parents to chaperone the trip.

Lizzie quietly said, "I'm not giving my mom the letter. She'll want to come. It's too embarrassing!"

"My dad's cool," Eric said. "I hope he comes." Eric's dad was the high school football coach.

Then Ms. Lilly asked, "Who has been to see King Tut at the museum already?"

Daisy raised her hand and waved it a little. Jason, Nick, Amber, and Tessa all raised their hands, too.

"Fantastic!" Ms. Lilly said. "You five will be my fabulous tour guides." Then she gave

each tour guide a special badge with a blank space where they could write their name. She told them they would need to stay after school Monday for tour guide training. Daisy was sooo excited!

"I hope you get to be my tour guide," Blanca said.

"Me too!" Daisy agreed.

5
Abuela Makes a Plan

Daisy could hardly wait until Monday! She wanted to know what Ms. Lilly was going to say at the meeting after school.

Thursday seemed like the longest day ever. Most of the kids brought their permission slips. A few kids were really mad because their parents were going to chaperone.

Daisy was kind of glad her mother would be working. Ms. Lilly was counting the number of parents who would be going.

"Very good, very good," Ms. Lilly said. "But, we need one more chaperone. Let's think outside of the box, my super smart superstars. You can ask grandparents, aunts, uncles, or older brothers and sisters."

Blanca said, "I don't have anyone I can ask. Both of my parents work and my grandparents live too far away."

Daisy said, "All my *tios* and *tias* work and my abuela takes care of Carmen all day."

Ms. Lilly began their day. They worked on their Egypt projects all morning. Then after lunch, they shared their color poems. Finally, it was time to go home.

That night during dinner, Daisy mentioned that Ms. Lilly still needed one more chaperone.

"I would ask to take the day off," Mami said, "but Principal Donaldson has so much work for me to do. Being a new principal isn't easy."

Paola said, "I want to go to see King Tut again. Can sisters come, too?"

"No *hermanas*," Daisy answered. "Sorry, Paola." Abuela's eyes were twinkling.

"I see you over there planning something, Mama," Papi said. Papi always called Abuela *Mama*.

Abuela said, "Oh Jorge, you always are thinking I am up to some kind of mischief. I am just thinking of going to the kitchen to get the flan."

At the mention of dessert, Manuel and Diego began chanting, "We're done! We're done!"

Daisy looked at their bare plates. They really were done, but they always ate everything on their plates and then had seconds and sometimes even thirds.

Mami was feeding Carmen. She said, "Boys, clear the plates so we have room to eat Abuela's delicious flan!"

After everyone stuffed themselves full of the creamy, sweet flan, they went to watch television while the boys did the dishes. Paola was glad the girls did not have to do dishes on

a night when Abuela made dessert. Dessert meant too many extra dishes to wash!

Soon it was time to get ready for bed. The girls could hear Mami singing to Carmen.

The next morning, Daisy woke up to something sticky on her face. Sitting on her stomach was her little, black dog, Noche. She had doggie slobber all over her face.

"Noche, get down!" Daisy said, giggling. "You're not an alarm clock."

Paola was laughing. She'd probably been watching Noche lick Daisy's face and didn't stop her because she thought it was funny.

Daisy washed her face and brushed her teeth. The girls got dressed quickly and went to the kitchen for breakfast.

Soon enough, lunch boxes were picked up and the Martinez kids were out the door to walk to school.

Daisy was glad it was Friday. There were only two more days until Monday. Blanca and DeShaye were waiting with Min at the lockers.

"You're so lucky!" Min said. "We have to go to the Environmental Center on our field trip. I like it, but we've taken the same field trip three years in a row now. I want to go somewhere else."

DeShaye nodded in agreement. "I am not wastin' my time going there another year,"

she said. "I have a tennis tournament next weekend, so I won't be here next Friday."

Daisy and Blanca were quiet. They knew they were lucky. Every day in Ms. Lilly's class was super fun! They didn't want to rub it in.

In room 210, the students were working in groups on their projects. Lola had been doing research on ancient Egypt. She made a list of all of the important places.

Eric had found a map of Egypt on the computer. They would use it as a model for making their map. Lola wanted to use brown ink to draw the lines and mark the cities.

Daisy thought the paper should look old. They asked Ms. Lilly for a giant piece of white bulletin board paper. It looked too new, too white! Daisy would have to think of a way to age the paper so it looked more like papyrus. Papyrus was a kind of paper made out of plants that people in ancient Egypt used.

Blanca's group was having a lot of fun. They were making a clay pot, some jewelry, and a carved walking staff. Blanca was making the jewelry and Raymond was making the staff. Most of the groups were working pretty hard.

The morning flew by and soon it was time for lunch. In the cafeteria, the kids were all happy. Fridays were pizza days. Daisy wished she didn't bring her lunch on pizza days.

"Want a bite?" Blanca offered as she pushed a piece of cheesy, pepperoni pizza toward her. Daisy did want a bite, but she said, "No thanks! I couldn't eat just a bite. I would have to eat a whole slice."

Raymond had two lunch trays. With his mouth full of pizza he said, "You can have a slice of my pizza, Daisy."

All of the girls looked at Raymond. DeShaye said, "Girl, you've got to be kidding! Raymond share food?"

Daisy thanked Raymond and reached for the piece of pizza. Blanca started to laugh.

"What's so funny?" Daisy asked.

"Oh, nothing," Blanca said. Daisy thought Blanca was being weird, but the pizza was yummy anyway.

After lunch they went to recess. Usually, the boys played with a soccer ball and the girls stood around talking to each other.

Today, Madison and Lizzie were being nice. They came to talk to Daisy and her friends. They were all taking about some television show where people sing and get prizes. Lizzie and Madison discussed who should win.

Daisy was getting bored. She saw Lola by the swings, so she said, "I really need to talk to Lola about our project. Sorry!" Then she walked over to the swings.

"Hey, Lola, about the map," Daisy said. "I'm going to ask my abuela how to get the paper to look kind of brown."

Lola said, "Wow! That's a great idea!"

A few minutes later, Daisy saw Raymond coming toward her with a volleyball in his hands. She remembered offering to help him with his serve.

He shouted, "Daisy, I have a ball so we can practice!"

Daisy looked around to see if she could find DeShaye. She saw Madison laughing and pointing at her and Raymond.

A few minutes later, Daisy and DeShaye began to practice serving with Raymond.

"Raymond, make sure your wrist is flat," Daisy said.

DeShaye said, "Boy, your arm is all over the place! Calm down. Focus on the ball."

"He serves like a girl!" Eric yelled.

DeShaye yelled back, "This girl is gonna come over there and make you sorry if you don't be nice!"

Eric turned and went to the other end of the field.

Soon it was time to go inside, but Raymond seemed to be getting better at serving. He said, "Thanks, Daisy!"

DeShaye said, "Are you forgetting who was really teaching you something?"

Raymond said, "Oh, right. Thanks, DeShaye."

That afternoon, while everyone was reading *The Egypt Game,* someone knocked on the door. When Ms. Lilly answered it, the person gave her a note.

Daisy noticed that whatever was in the note made her teacher super happy.

"I have some great news!" Ms. Lilly announced. "We just got a new volunteer and now we have enough chaperones. Daisy's grandmother will be coming with us to visit King Tut."

Daisy was in shock. Who would watch Carmen? Daisy knew she had to hurry home after school and find out!

That afternoon when Daisy got home, she shouted anxiously, "Abuela? Abuela?" Then she ran into her tiny grandmother coming out of the kitchen with a snack for them.

"Sí, mi ja," Abuela said.

"Something happened today at school and I think it is a mistake," Daisy said in a rush. "Abuela, did you say you are going to go on our field trip to the museum?"

Abuela grinned. She answered, "Sí."

"If you go, then who will take care of Carmen?" Daisy asked.

Abuela explained that Mami had talked to Ms. Lilly. Her ***maestra*** agreed that since

Carmen was such a little baby Abuela could bring her along.

Paola had been quietly listening, and she began to pout. She whined, "I thought you said no hermanas, Daisy."

Daisy was starting to panic. What would the kids at school think?

That night at dinner, Daisy tried to convince Mami that Abuela should not go on the field trip.

As they passed the plates of chicken ***mole*** and rice Daisy said, "Mami, I don't think that Abuela should go on the trip to the museum. Pushing the stroller all over the museum would be too much work for her."

Papi started to laugh. He said, "Mama, I do not think you were planning on just getting the flan last night after all!"

"Oh, Jorge, I like to help," Abuela said. "That is all."

Daisy continued, "There are too many stairs and you would have to take the elevator. Then you would not be with my class. A chaperone stays with the class, right?"

Abuela beamed and said, "Daisy, do not worry. I have thought of everything. I will not bring the stroller."

Daisy frowned again, looking confused. Abuela said, "I will carry our sweet Carmen in a *rebozo*."

A rebozo was like a giant scarf or shawl. Women in Mexico folded them into a triangle and tied them over their shoulder to cradle a baby like a sling.

We are not in Mexico, Daisy thought. Then she felt ashamed. She loved Abuela and Carmen.

Daisy did the dishes quickly with Paola. Then she called Blanca.

As soon as she answered, Daisy blurted out, "Blanca, my abuela is coming on the field trip and she is bringing Carmen! I thought it was just a mistake!"

Blanca said, "So what? I like your grandmother and Carmen is cute."

"I know," Daisy said. "But the other kids will think it's weird. I just know it! Madison will make fun of us. Abuela is going to carry Carmen in a rebozo."

Blanca said, "Well, that is different, but not to us. Just pretend it's normal."

When they got off the phone, Daisy thought about her friend's advice. She decided it was the best plan after all.

Daisy thought, *I'll act like everything is okay and maybe no one will notice that I brought my grandmother and a baby to the museum with me.* Daisy wasn't too convinced.

All weekend Daisy thought about her meeting Monday with Ms. Lilly. She was still worried about the field trip. She imagined everyone asking questions about the little old woman in the bright skirt with the baby.

"Who is that? Is that old lady with us? Why does she have a baby?" they would ask. Daisy decided she would just keep quiet.

7 On the Road

At the end of the day Monday, Ms. Lilly said, "I need my tour guides to stay, please." Daisy did not need a reminder!

Daisy, Jason, Nick, Amber, and Tessa all moved to the table in the back of the room. Ms. Lilly had some folders ready. On the front they said, "Tour Guide Packet."

Daisy was starting to feel excited about the field trip again! Nick couldn't wait for Ms. Lilly. He opened his folder.

"Wow! This is so cool," Nick said.

"I think we should wait for Ms. Lilly," Jason told the group. Just then, Ms. Lilly flew through the door. She had taken the rest of the class out to the bus loop for dismissal.

"Nick, you are getting ahead of us!" she said when she saw Nick with his folder open.

Ms. Lilly explained that each folder had maps, notes, and a special scavenger hunt for that group.

"On the day of the trip, you will wear your badge and carry a staff," Ms. Lilly said. She held up a stick painted gold with a large sunburst on the top.

"I chose the sun because Ra is the Egyptian sun god," she explained. "Everyone can see the sun, and with your staff all of the super smart students in your group should be able to see their leader at all times."

When she asked if anyone had any questions, Jason asked, "Ms. Lilly, how do we know which students are in our group?"

"No problemo!" she said. Then she gave each guide a list of five students in their group.

She told them that they could choose a name for their group.

Jason said, "I call owls!"

"I guess I'll stick with cobras," Daisy said. Since her group had Lizzie, Nick, Pablo, and Lola she thought the cobras was a good fit.

The next few days were busy. The class was trying to finish reading *The Egyptian Game*. And they added to their poetry portfolios. They worked on a who am I poem, a shape poem, and a limerick.

On Wednesday, Ms. Lilly said, "Okay, super smart superstars. You can do a haiku for extra credit homework. Direction sheets are on my desk."

Daisy didn't need extra credit, but she took one anyway. Eric took one, too. He probably needed the points. He did not turn in his cloud poem.

On Thursday afternoon, Ms. Lilly said, "Class, tomorrow you will need to either bring your lunch or the cafeteria will provide a sack lunch for you. Also, make sure you wear comfortable shoes."

Then she announced the groups. Raymond was in Madison's group with Tessa. Madison said, "Ms. Lilly, you know Raymond and I can't stand each other! How could you let this happen?"

Ms. Lilly allowed Raymond to switch places with Nick. That seemed to make Madison happy, but the strange part was Raymond seemed really happy, too. Usually he didn't care about anything.

Finally, Friday arrived and the students from room 210 went to board the field trip bus at nine thirty. Ms. Lilly had on a tan suit with a hat that had a white net on the top of it.

"Ms. Lilly looks like she's going on a safari," Daisy said.

Jason replied, "No, she looks like she'd going to an archaeology dig."

Ms. Lilly had a clipboard with student names and emergency numbers. She also had a first aid kit. Ms. Lilly liked to be prepared for anything.

Once they were all on the bus, Ms. Lilly explained that the chaperones would follow the bus in their own cars. Daisy was glad. Carmen needed her car seat, so this worked out better.

During the ride, Daisy looked at the scavenger hunt sheets again. There were ten questions for each team. They were all the same. Daisy wanted her team to be ready!

The King Tut Scavenger Hunt

1. Who found King Tut? ______________

2. According to superstition, the mummy's curse killed a pet and a friend. Name them.

____

3. How many coffins did King Tut have?

____

4. Why was the last coffin a sight to behold? It was made of ________.

5. What did kings wear: earrings, jewels, or sandals? ____________________

6. What goddess is part lion, part crocodile, and part hippopotamus? ______________

7. What is King Tut's mask made of? ______

8. What was the name of ancient Egyptian writing? ______________

9. What year was King Tut's tomb found? ______

10. How many soldiers were buried with King Tut? __________

8
The Hunt Begins

Once the students arrived at the museum, they were joined by their chaperones. Abuela came to stand quietly by Daisy. She smelled like cinnamon. Early that morning she had made *churros*. They were kind of like cookies, but better.

Carmen was sleeping in the deep blue rebozo hanging over her grandmother's shoulder. She didn't make a peep. Madison kept staring at Daisy's abuela, but Daisy went with the plan and acted like everything was normal.

Daisy introduced her grandmother to Lizzie, Raymond, Pablo, and Lola.

"Hola, friends of Daisy," Abuela said with a smile.

Surprisingly Lizzie said, "Your grandma is nice. I wish my grandma lived closer so I could see her."

"My grandma lives in Puerto Rico," Pablo said. "I never get to see her."

Daisy was starting to see how lucky she was. Then Raymond said, "My grandmother died last year."

Abuela said, "Today, I will be your abuela too, Raymond." Raymond looked very happy.

Daisy told her group to pull out their tickets. She moved to the front of her line with her sun staff. She was wearing her badge and knew all the questions for the scavenger hunt.

Once everyone was inside, Daisy gave the paper to Lola for her to write the answers on. They could not divide up and look around. Ms. Lilly insisted each group stay together. The group that found the most correct answers would win a prize.

Eric's dad was clapping his hands and shouting, "We're gonna win this thing! Right, team?" They all said, "Yes!" Then he shouted, "I can't hear you!"

Someone working at the museum tapped him on the shoulder. When he turned to look, the museum worker put a finger over his lips and said, "Sssh!"

Daisy thought it was awkward having your dad get in trouble at the museum, but Eric didn't seem to care.

In the first room, Daisy's group saw many photographs of the mummy's tomb. Pablo found some black-and-white pictures of Howard Carter, the famous archaeologist who discovered King Tut's tomb.

Daisy said, "Good work, Pablo! Lola, write it down."

"I'm on it, Daisy!" Lola said. Daisy smiled. Everything seemed to be going pretty good.

In the next room, they saw amazing painted chests and couches with animal heads carved on them. One couch had lions, another had cows. The last one had an animal that was part lion, crocodile, and hippopotamus.

The strange animal was supposed to be the goddess Ammut. It was another one of their questions. Lola wrote it down, too.

In the third room, they saw many treasures. The Egyptians were great artists. They made beautiful jewelry. Daisy noticed her abuela swinging the rebozo. Carmen was awake.

Daisy wondered if she would cry and then they would get in trouble for making too much noise. Raymond was sticking close to Abuela. He seemed to like talking to her. Daisy wondered what they were talking about.

Then, Lizzie pulled Daisy's arm and pointed to a fancy jar with a carved lid. The tiny card in front of it said that it was for the king's face cream. Both girls put a hand over their mouth as they laughed.

“Things were different back then I guess,” Lizzie said. “Did you see those earrings?”

“I did,” Daisy answered. “And they were worn by men and women!”

Lola said, “My brother wants to pierce his ear and my dad won’t let him do it!”

In the last chamber, they saw the coffins. There were four of them. Abuela said, “Look, the last one is gold.”

Lola said, “Hey, you found the answer to one of the questions, Mrs. Martinez.”

Daisy’s group all crowded around the mask of King Tut. It was solid gold, too. Tut had a long, funny beard that looked like the braid in Daisy’s hair, but shorter.

When they looked at an actual mummy Lola said, “Eww, gross!” Pablo thought it was really awesome and looked like beef jerky.

“Yuck!” Lizzie said. “I’m glad I never eat beef jerky!”

The whole group enjoyed looking around some more. There were so many things to look at and read.

Abuela was reading everything. Sometimes she asked Raymond what a word meant. This made Raymond feel important. He liked helping Daisy's grandmother. She was really nice and she told him she brought treats for after lunch, too!

Eric's group was getting in trouble again for being too loud. Blanca waved from the other side of the room and did a thumbs-up in Daisy's direction.

Finally, the class made their way to the exhibit exit. Right outside, Ms. Lilly told them they could look in the gift shop for fifteen minutes and then they would go outside to the garden to eat their lunches.

The gift shop had some cool pencils with hieroglyphics on them. Daisy picked one out with an eye on it. It reminded her of the

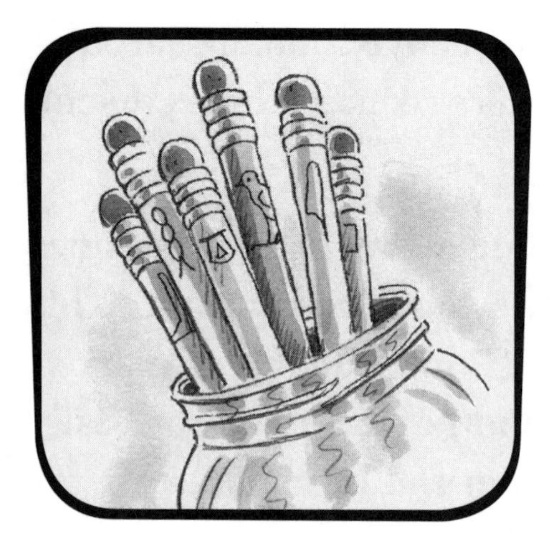

first clue Ms. Lilly gave them about their field trip. She also got a pencil that looked like a staff.

Right outside the gift shop was a machine with hieroglyphics all over it. If you put a dollar in it, you could get a cartouche of your name.

Usually a cartouche is oval with a royal name written in hieroglyphics. Daisy really wanted one with her name, but she already spent her money.

Raymond put his dollar in and typed his name. Daisy watched. He said, "I like your grandma."

"Thanks!" Daisy said. "Your cartouche is so cool. I wish I had one."

Raymond asked, "Want mine?"

"No, it has your name on it," Daisy said. "But thanks anyway."

Out in the museum garden, everyone began to eat lunch. Abuela sat on a bench in the shade with Carmen. She was awake now and making little baby noises.

A lot of the girls in Daisy's class were standing around her grandmother looking at Carmen.

"Daisy, your baby sister is so cute!" Amber said. The other girls were saying that Carmen's pink dress was pretty, that her fingers were so tiny, and her hair so curly.

Carmen cooed like she understood and was trying to say thank you.

Lola said, "I think she's smart, too. Can you hear her talking?"

"It's just baby talk," Madison said. "It doesn't mean anything!"

Lizzie said, "Oh, Madison, come look at her. She's really sweet." Madison planned to say something mean, but Carmen's little mouth made a tiny smile. Abuela told Madison that meant Carmen liked her.

Madison begged, "Can I hold Carmen? Pleeease?" Daisy thought, *Wow! Maybe Carmen has superpowers! She made Madison smile and say, "Hey this baby is smart!"*

Abuela called Daisy and Raymond over and gave them each a paper sack filled with cinnamon churros to pass out. The kids in room 210 loved them. They asked if they could have more.

"Of course!" Abuela said. "I always make enough for more." Daisy saw Raymond was passing some out, eating some, passing some more out, and eating even more!

Soon, Ms. Lilly asked them to join their groups and make sure they had recorded all their scavenger hunt answers. Daisy's group was only missing one answer. She knew that supposedly the curse killed Carter's partner Lord Carnavon, but she did not know anything about a pet.

"Did anyone read anything about a pet that died?" Daisy asked.

Abuela said, "Raymond helped me read that part! It was a pet canary."

Raymond added, "Yeah, and a cobra killed it." Lola wrote it down.

Ms. Lilly said, "Do we have a team with all of the answers?"

Jason said, "We have them all!"

Daisy said, "We do, too!"

Ms. Lilly was delighted. She said, "I think we have two teams tied for first place. I have pharaoh hats for the Owls and the Cobras."

Eric's dad groaned. He did not like losing. Then Ms. Lilly said, "You can explore the rest

of the museum, but meet me at the bus at one thirty. Don't be late!"

On the ride back to school, all of the kids were talking about the museum. Daisy was busy thinking about her awesome abuela. Blanca was right—everything worked out fine. Actually it was terrific.

Raymond was sitting in the seat behind Daisy. He tapped Daisy on the head with a small roll of paper. Then he handed it to her.

"What's this?" Daisy asked. Blanca said, "Open it and see."

Daisy unrolled the paper and saw a hand, eagle, reed, bolt, and another reed. It was a cartouche.

"Raymond, your cartouche is awesome!" Daisy said.

But, Raymond shrugged and said, "That one is too short to say *Raymond*. It says *Daisy*." His face was a little red as he held up his for Daisy to see.

Daisy said, "Thanks, Raymond!"

Raymond said, "No problem. You helped me with my volleyball serve."

Ms. Lilly turned in her seat to face the kids. She said, "Students, you won't believe what I have planned for us next! Let me say, it will be some celebration."

Daisy already had a clue. Monday she had noticed that Ms. Lilly had a small Christmas tree, an Easter basket, a menorah, and a box full of other things under her the table in the back of the room.

Daisy thought about asking Ms. Lilly about the clues, but for today she just wanted to get home and give her abuela a great big hug. Oh, and Carmen too! It had been a super cool trip. Her abuela was a superstar!

abuela – grandmother
churros – crispy cinnamon treat
como me gustan las palabras – I like the words
escuela – school
frijoles – kidney beans
hermana – sister
maestra – teacher
mi ja – my dear
mole – a spice sauce made with chilies and chocolate
Muy hermoso – very beautiful
por favor – please
sí – yes
tamale – dough rolled with meat or beans and wrapped with corn husks
tia – aunt
tio – uncle